Bruna

by Anne Cottringer

illustrations by
Gillian McClure

BLOOMSBURY
CHILDREN'S
BOOKS

For Alex and Holly – AC

To Marcus and Polly – GM^{c}C

Text copyright © Anne Cottringer 2003
Illustrations copyright © Gillian McClure 2003

First U.S. Edition 2003
Published by Bloomsbury, New York and London
Distributed to the trade by Holtzbrinck Publishers
Library of Congress Cataloging-in-Publication Data
Bruna / by Anne Cottringer; illustrations by Gillian McClure.
p. cm.
Summary: Bruna, a girl who lives in a hut all alone, tries everything she can think of to keep from being cold,
but nothing works until she discovers the warmth of friendship.
ISBN 1-58234-836-7 (alk. paper)
[1. Cold--Fiction. 2. Bears--Fiction. 3. Friendship--Fiction.] I. McClure, Gillian, ill. II. Title
PZ7.C82967 Br 2003
[E]--dc21
2002028340

Printed in Hong Kong by South China Printing Co.

1 3 5 7 9 10 8 6 4 2

Bloomsbury USA Children's Books
175 Fifth Avenue
New York, New York 10010

There was once a girl named Bruna.

She lived in a little hut all by herself and she was always cold.

In spring when everyone else was throwing off their winter coats, she

kept her buttons done up and her woolly hat pulled down over her ears.

In summer when
everyone splashed in
the river under the hot
sun, Bruna sat alone on
the bank wrapped up
in her woolly overcoat.

In autumn, she watched
the birds fly south to
find warmer weather
and she knew it was
time to get out her
extra-long scarf.

In winter she wore mittens all the time, even indoors. She piled logs high on the fire, turned up the central heating and read her book with five hot water bottles next to her. Still she was cold.

She tried eating Red Hot Fireballs – "a sweet with guaranteed heat," said the packet – but they only burnt the inside of her mouth, and turned her tongue bright red.

A SWEET WITH GUARL HEAT

She tried to work up a sweat by running across the fields like Fleet the wild pony.

But her muscles ached to bursting before she ever felt any warmth.

She followed the birds south to the warmth of Africa. Bruna stayed with them for a week and got a sunburned nose, but she was still freezing the entire time.

Heat lamps, steam baths, tropical islands, hot curry – nothing seemed to make Bruna warm.

One morning, back at home, Bruna was just
waking up under her pile of eighteen blankets,
two duvets and a rug, when she heard a voice
calling from outside. "Help! Help!" cried
the voice.

Bruna looked out of the window. Someone
was thrashing about in the river. "Help! Help!"
cried the voice again.

Bruna ran out of the door toward the river.
The voice belonged to a big brown bear who
was about to go under the water.

Bruna looked at the icy water. She shivered.
"Help!" cried the bear.

Bruna picked up a long stick. She felt the cold clamp around her ankles as she waded into the icy water.

"Grab this!" she shouted. The bear reached for it, but missed.

Bruna waded further into the freezing water. She felt the cold squeezing her waist. The bear made another grab and missed again.

Bruna waded in up to her chest. She felt the cold beating against her heart. She stretched out over the water.

The bear made one last grab and this time held on.
Bruna pulled with all her strength and hauled the
big, shivering bear out of the water.

"I thought bears could swim," said Bruna.

"Most can," said the bear. "But I can't."

Back in her hut, Bruna tucked the bear
under her pile of eighteen blankets, two
duvets, and a rug. She piled logs on the
fire. She turned up the central heating.

"What's your name?" asked Bruna.

"Ursa," replied the bear.

"I'll warm you up with some hot soup," said Bruna. She took off her mittens to make the soup and was surprised to find that her fingers weren't as numb as usual.

"Delicious soup!" said Ursa, and she threw off the rug.

"I'll read you a story with a heart-warming ending,"
said Bruna. She took off her scarf so she could speak
the words, and was surprised that she didn't feel chilly.
"Lovely story," said Ursa, and threw off the two duvets.

"I'll play you a hot tune on the piano," said Bruna.
She took off her coat to reach the keys and was
surprised that she didn't start shivering.

"Shake, rattle and roll!" laughed Ursa, and she
threw off all the blankets.

"Let's go out and play!" cried Bruna.

Bruna and Ursa swung from the big tree. Bruna took off her woolly sweater.

They played tag in the woods. Bruna took off her woolly socks.

They tickled the sunfish in the river.
And Bruna took off her woolly hat.

By the end of the day,
Bruna was running
around barefoot.

Ursa stayed and played
and learned to swim.

Bruna never felt cold again. Now, on very cold winter days, it's Ursa who sometimes gets the shivers. Then Bruna snuggles up close to keep her warm.

"Who would have thought I could ever be anyone's hot water bottle!" says Bruna, as she smiles and snuggles up even closer.